I0846899

# The Mystical House

# Heaven on Earth

Author

DeiAdra NiCoLe

# TABLE OF CONTENTS

## Contents

# INTRODUCTION

In this fictitious short story, we will unravel the mystery surrounding an abandoned home and its occupants. The home was built in the 1970's and is located on the outskirts of a tiny Polish village. The home is known as "The Mystical House" for its bazaar activities. The home is the center of the town's debate, as it has the town in an uproar. Many of the townspeople feel the home is a blessing, while others view it as a curse. It goes without debate that it is anything except an ordinary home.

In this fictitious short story, we will be delving into the mysteries surrounding an old, abandoned home. The home is located at 333 Lovejoy Road. It is located in one of the most exclusive communities on the outskirts of Poland.

The home that now sets vacant was built in the early 70's. It is often referred to as "*The Mystical House*." The home is one of the oldest homes in the town. The house is listed among the town's historic homes. The residents of the town claim that the abandoned home was originally a field used as a place of worship by the Indians.

# HISTORY OF THE MEDICAL FACILITY

The son of an Australian family, during his tour of duty, helicopter was shot down while flying over the area. Amazingly, the soldier lived through the crash, dying hours later. The closest hospital to the town was more than two hours away. The family was devastated when they learned of the tragedy. They were committed to ensuring that the past never repeated itself. The family bought the property on which they intended to erect a medical facility. In memory of their son and other fallen heroes, the medical center was constructed. Although the medical center was built in honor of the warriors, it wasn't just for veterans.

The town's people and individuals of low-income status also utilized the medical facility. The medical center was operated from donations. It was made up of three floors which consisted of thirty rooms and twenty-five bathrooms. The facility was built up on a hill. It is said the facility was purposely built on top of the hill for better visibility for emergencies. The family of the fallen hero often visited the facility. They donated monetary gifts, along with food and clothing items. Medical supplies were routinely donated from other medical facilities. Allied health professionals worked on a voluntary basis volunteering their services.

The facility was a blessing to those individuals that could not afford to pay the regular prices for their medications and hospital visits. They were seen by some of the best physicians in the practice. Doctors from various specialties such as family medicine, cardiology, internal medicine, neurosurgery to name a few volunteered their services. The people depended on the facility and its physicians to satisfy their medical needs. Many patients had established a rapport with several of the physicians working in the medical facility. The medical center had been in operation for fifteen years. During the fifteen-year time span several miracles were witnessed at the facility.

Many patients had come to the medical center with terminal illnesses such as stage four cancer, dementia, along with other degenerative or deteriorating conditions. All of which left the facility completely healed from their illnesses. Regardless of the type of illness they battled. They all received a clean bill of health. Ninety percent of the patients who are brought into the center in critical condition recovers. The center has only lost one patient in the fifteen years it has been in operation. The patient was an elderly man who died from natural causes. It was rare that a physician or any allied health personnel would acquire any sickness or illnesses of any sort from a patient.

Although many physicians and allied personnel worked on a voluntary basis. As donations began to come in, they were given a salary. All allied health care staff were well taken care of and wanted for nothing. The donations and grants received by the center made it the highest paying medical facility in the area. They had the luxury of using the latest in technology. The staff were blessed beyond measure for using their God-given talents to help those less fortunate. The staff received lavish gifts such as electronics, automobiles, and exquisite trips. They were like an extended family. They enjoyed working together and frequently spent time together outside of work.

# THE RESURRECTION OF THE MYSTICAL HOUSE

The fallen hero was said to have been the couple's only child. After the death of the soldier's parents, the medical center was taken over and run by a distant cousin. He made the decision to renovate the facility a month after taking control of it. He informed the staff that the facility would be closed for the remodifications until further notice. The center was closed for several months for the upgrades. Upon the completion of the center's renovations he was pleasantly surprised with the results. He was overwhelmingly surprised that he decided to make it his personal home.

What had formerly been a medical center designed to save lives was now a luxurious home setting up on a hill. The home was elegantly and gracefully designed. The color of the home was beige with violet hues with gold accents. Rumor had it that the inside decor was also beige and violet with gold accents. The outside furnishings such as patio chairs were also violet and beige with gold trimmings down to the mailbox. In front of the home stood a seven-foot gold plated waterfall. Three months later, after the completion of the home's renovation, the homeowner disappeared never to be seen again.

This marked the beginning of several disappearances involving the home as it would gain its name *The Mystical House.* The inside furnishings were said to have been in excellent condition and didn't appear to have ever been used. Some items were said to have still been in boxes. Several failed attempts were made to reach out to the homeowner and other relatives to discuss the future of the home. There were rumors that the owner of the home, had become gravely ill. He was said to have returned to his native homeland where he settled until his untimely death. In one instance a lady claiming to be the aunt of the fallen soldier was reached via phone.

After learning that the call was in reference to the home located at 333 Lovejoy Road, she immediately disconnected the call. She was never heard from again. All other attempts have ended in dead end leads. It was eventually decided upon by the state to rent out the home in an attempt to assist with its property taxes. The home was vacant ninety percent of the time. No one was able to live in the home for more than a year. The one tenant who actually lived in the home for a year worked out of state and was never at the residence. The tenants either moved out of the home or vanished in thin air never to be seen again. Throughout the years dozens of people were reported missing.

Sixty percent of the individuals that were reported missing in the town were reported to have been seen entering the residence at 333 Lovejoy Road. It was no secret that there was a connection between the house and the disappearance of its tenants. People were fearful of the house, refusing to live in it. The house throughout the fifty-four years of its existence has only housed a total of five families. The mystery surrounding the home caused it to gain global attention. It became the center of attention attracting millions of tourists yearly. Tourist came from all over the world to visit the home. It brought in thousands of dollars into the small town making the town famous because of *"The Mystical House."*

The home is known to either bring its visitors fortune or cause misfortune. The home became the center of the town's debate. Many of the towns' people to include law makers, had mixed emotions about the home.

The house being the center of controversy leaving many of the town's people divided. Many felt as if the house was a blessing while others felt it was a curse. Some of the town's people have even gone as far as to call the house haunted. While others have testified that the home has brought them good fortune, changing their lives for the better. Some of the residents wanted to see the home demolished. While others wanted to turn it back into a medical facility.

# THE COMMITTEE MEETING

A select few wanted to preserve the home as a part of the town's history. Lawmakers to include the town's mayor. Mayor Michael Seahawk were undecided about the Mystical House. The home wasn't a candidate for demolition. It was well kept and were one of the most beautiful homes in the town. It were also on the town's historic list. Guidelines states any property listed as a historic property must first be removed from the list before it can be demolished or renovated. The only exception to the rule were if the owner(s) of the property decided to renovate or demolish the property themself.

Elected officials will meet with the town's people where they will decide on the fate of *The Mystical House*. Each member of the committee's life has in some way been significantly impacted by *The Mystical House*. Many of them have volunteered to share their life altering experiences involving the home.

More than fifty percent of the town attended the meeting. Mayor Michael Seahawk, Henry Ashcraft, Jerry Nuttz was among other city leaders and towns people that decided to share their stories. Mayor Seahawk is called upon first to share his experience involving *The Mystical House*. Mayor Seahawk approaches the podium.

# THE SEAHAWKS DISAPPEARANCE

He glances up briefly at the ceiling with tears in his eyes as he tries to keep his composure. The mayor clears his throat as he prepares to share his story with audience. He stares into the crowd as he begins to speak to the audience. I can recall the events as if it were yesterday. It was the morning of April 01, 2019, as the mayor, his wife Jennifer and their son Jaylyn awoke and prepared to start their day. Jennifer prepared breakfast for the family to include her signature famous homemade cinnamon rolls. Michael noticed during breakfast that Jennifer seemed anxious as she sat working on her computer.

Jennifer worked diligently as she prepared for her presentation. Michael began to questioned Jennifer about the project while offering his assistance. She was overwhelmed with excitement. She begun to explain to Michael that they could possibly be the next owners of *The Mystical House*. Jennifer was a local realtor who was very fond of *The Mystical House*. She frequently referred to it as her "dream home." She felt that it was something special about the home. Jennifer tells Michael that she plans to get the approval to purchase the home. Michael thinks that she's just talking until he realizes that she is serious. She began to show him the paperwork where she had begun the process.

Jennifer tells him that she would like to make the home their personal home. She feels that *The Mystical House* would be a great investment. Michael doesn't feel optimistic about her purchasing the home knowing the home's history. Jennifer tells Michael that she has already been preapproved. She tells Michael that her last task is to visit the home to take pictures to submit with her proposal. Jennifer hopes to get the approval for the home to be removed from the town's list of historical properties. Michael is furious with Jennifer for not consulting him before making such a major decision. A decision that could negatively affect their finances along with their lives in general.

Michael confides in Jennifer that he feels uneasy about the project. He feels she could be making a serious mistake. Michael feels that Jennifer was selfish in her actions. He advises her to abandon the project. Jennifer insists on overseeing the project through to its completion. Jennifer and Michael get into a heated argument. She finally throws her hands up telling him that she must leave for work. The couple decides they will revisit the issue when she returns home. Jennifer and Jaylyn, the couple's son heads out to work and school. Michael leaves a short time later heading to his office. Shortly after arriving at work Michael gets a call from Good Cents Realty.

The real estate company that employes Jennifer. Lou-Anne the office manager is inquiring about Jennifer. She worried that Jennifer had not shown up for work nor had she called. Lou-Anne claimed they had called Jennifer's phone several times throughout the morning. However, their messages were sent to her voicemail. Michael immediately phones Jennifer but gets her voicemail. He rushes home to see if she had returned home. When he arrived at their home there was no sign of Jennifer. Everything were just as they had left it earlier. Michael curiously called Jaylyn's school to see if she had taken him to school.

The school's administrator confirmed with Michael that

Jaylyn had not shown up for school. Michael began to panic

he knows Jennifer and knows that this wasn't like her.

Jennifer enjoyed her job as a real estate agent. She had won

several accolades and was known as one of the best agents

around town. She was adamant about Jaylyn not missing any

days out of school for any reason. Michael could sense that

something was wrong. Michael knew that Jennifer was

considering buying the home located at 333 Lovejoy Road.

He decided to visit the home to see if he spotted Jennifer's

car. After arriving at the home, he was relieved when he did

not see Jennifer's car.

This now presents the question if Jennifer and Jaylyn's disappearance could be the result of foul play.

 Michael returned home where he phoned the police for help. Law officials turned to the public for assistance. Law officials aired Jennifer and Jaylyn's photographs on the local news cast. They were requesting for anyone with information about Jennifer and Jaylyn's disappearance to come forward. Shortly after the airing of the telecast they got an anonymous tip. The caller reported he saw Jennifer's car parked in the driveway of a nearby home. The home was located a few blocks from the couple's home. As the officers are traveling to the address provided by the caller Jennifer's vehicle comes speeding past them.

# HENRY'S TESTIMONY

The officers instantly turn around and start to pursue

the driver of the vehicle. The driver without hesitation pulls

over and cooperates fully with the authorities. The suspect is

none other than the town's drunk, a homeless man by the

name of Henry. He is booked and taken into custody for

(DUI) driving under the influence. (Mayor Seahawk before

being moved to tears passes the microphone to Henry

Ashcraft.) Henry finishes the story telling how he was

questioned by law officials about how he acquired Jennifer

Seahawk's vehicle. Henry tells the officers he was walking

down Lovejoy Road when that the driver of the vehicle

approached him asking for help.

The driver subsequently introduced herself as Jennifer Seahawk and her son Jaylyn. The car was parked-on side of the road in front of *The Mystical House* with the hood raised. Henry told officers after checking underneath the hood of the car it was discovered that the car had a busted hose.

The car had lost its fluids resulting in its over-heating. Henry told officers the driver offered to pay him to fix the automobile. Jennifer provided Henry with cash as agreed upon along with the keys to the vehicle. Henry claims Jennifer told him that she and Jaylyn would be inside the home taking photos. Henry tells officers that he warned Jennifer that entering the home could have some undesirable consequences.

Henry tells officers that Jennifer assured him that all would be well. Informing him that she had heard the story before. The Seahawks and Henry had agreed to meet in front of the home within an hour. According to Henry, he watched them as they entered and closed the door. Henry claims he departed from Jennifer and Jaylyn leaving them at *The Mystical House*. Henry left to purchase the necessary parts to repair the automobile. Henry says when he returned for Jenniffer and Jaylyn they were nowhere to be found. He tells the officers he knocked at the door of the home but never got an answer. When he tried to enter the home, the door was locked. He returned to the car, where he waited for over two hours, but they never came out of the home.

Officers asked Henry why he didn't report their

disappearance to the police. Henry told officers he was

reluctant to speak with authorities in fear of being blamed for

their disappearance. Henry afterwards began sobbing

uncontrollably. Henry tells Mayor Seahawk and officers that

he knows firsthand what the mayor must be going through.

Henry begins to share with them his encounter with the

Mystical House. Two years earlier, a similar incident

happened to him, causing him to lose his family.

Henry, now jobless and known as the town's drunk,

was once a hard worker and devoted family man. After

graduating from high school, he was offered a job at the tire

factory.

It was his first job. Henry was painfully shy and wasn't big on words. He worked alongside his life's companion, Helga, at the factory. Helga, on the other hand, was the opposite of Henry. Helga had a hearing impairment and as a result spoke very loudly. She was a social butterfly and could befriend anyone. Helga was well known for her nurturing ways. She often went out of her way to help others. When Helga and Henry met there was an instant attraction. According to Henry she was the most beautiful woman Henry had ever laid eyes on. She was everything that he could ask for in a companion. Helga was beautiful, she looked as if she was taken from the page of a magazine. She got Henry's attention in all the right ways.

Not to mention she was a wonderful cook considering

Henry didn't know how to cook. She was loving, charming,

and outgoing. She was fun and exciting she knew how to

have a good time. The pair complimented one another. Helga

knew how to bring Henry out of his shell. Henry knew how

to humble her. Henry desperately wanted to ask Helga out on

a date. He contemplated when would be the right time to ask

her out. He wondered if she felt the same way about him.

Henry and Helga sat together daily where they ate lunch with

mutual friends. One Friday at the conclusion of lunch the

girls asked Helga if she had plans for the weekend. They

wanted her to go out with them for a girl's night out.

Helga responded: I am sorry, but I have already made plans. Henry and I will be watching a movie over dinner at my place. Henry looked on in amusement. He was surprised but glad to hear Helga's response. While walking Helga back to her workstation, Henry inquired about the plans that she had made. Helga chuckled, explaining that she was only trying to let the girls down easy. She apologized to Henry for having to make him the scapegoat. Helga suddenly realized the look on Henry's face as his smile quickly turned into an upside-down frown. Henry, I am sorry, did you want to go out on a date? I didn't think that a date with me would pique your curiosity.

# FINANCIAL HARDSHIP

However, if you want to go, I would be delighted to go with you. Henry quickly nodded his head before answering, "Yes, I would love to go." The following night, Henry and Helga had dinner at Helga's place, followed by a movie. Henry and Helga became exclusive after dating for two months. They dated for a year before he asked her to marry him. A year after getting married, Helga came to learn that she was expecting the couple's first child. They were ecstatic to learn that they would be parents. The couple gave birth to two beautiful healthy babies. They had twins, a boy, and a girl, whom they named Alex and Alexandria. The couple decided it would be best for Helga to remain at home with the twins until they became old enough to attend school.

As time passed the couple began to struggle financially. She was left with no option but to return to work. Two weeks after returning to work, the company announced because business had slowed down, they would soon be laying off. Helga, a few days later, was laid off. Only having one paycheck coming into their home began to put a strain on the couple's finances. Although Helga received unemployment, it wasn't enough. She didn't have very long to receive it. She had received the majority of her unemployment during her maternity leave. Helga searched for alternative work opportunities. She knew that once she returned to work, they would have the responsibility of paying for childcare for the twins.

Conversely, if she stayed at home with them, they would not have enough money to cover all of their household expenses. The couple decided to have Helga remain at home with the twins. Henry got a second job to cover the remainder of the couple's expenses. The plant soon went bankrupt and was forced to close its doors indefinitely. Henry was left without a job depending only on his part-time job. Henry's part time job was at the local high school where he worked as a janitor. The couple was afraid of not being able to provide for their children and possibly losing their home. Henry began applying to other jobs in town but had no luck as the competition was now greater than ever. Henry took odd jobs on the side to be able to provide for their family.

# THE ABUSE

The stress of the couple's finances began to negatively affect their relationship. The couple began having disagreements daily which eventually became abusive. Henry's parents were older when they conceived him. Henry was the youngest of two children his older brother was a preacher just as Henry's father. His parents were married for thirty-five years. He had never witnessed his parents having a disagreement of any type. Henry hated chaos of any kind he was a very humble man. He was taught by his father that a man under any circumstances should never hit a woman.

He was a lot like his father, he was a very meek and mild-mannered person. He was one that rarely got out of character. Getting out of character for him was raising his voice two decimals higher than normal. In many instances suited him perfectly since he spoke softly. If he became angry, no one would ever know. He always had a smile on his face, even when he was upset. Helga, on the other hand, was the total opposite. She secretly battled with the inner demons of her past. She was from a broken home. Her mother and father had divorced when she was a toddler. Her mother had remarried twice afterwards. All of her mother's marriages ended in spousal abuse.

Helga had grown up in an abusive home. She had seen a lot growing up. She often found herself in uncompromising positions. In many instances she was forced to fight for her very own life. She often revisits the events in her head. Helga, just like her mother in adulthood, found herself in abusive relationships. She was confused as to why many of her past lovers told her they loved her but yet hit her. Helga normalized physical abuse as a component of all romantic relationships. She thought being physically abusive was a way of one expressing their love. Henry on the other hand was different from anyone she had ever dated. Although she openly praised Henry for not being like her past lovers. She loved him and questioned if he loved her.

It was no secret that he wasn't an abusive person nor was he towards her. Helga made the assumption that because he wasn't abusive, he didn't love her. She was baffled as to why he did not love her. After all she was the mother of his children and a great wife. Helga began drinking alcohol on a daily basis. She consumed large amounts of alcohol as a way to deal with her problems. When intoxicated, she became angry and belligerent. Helga frequently took out her aggression on Henry resulting in her being physically aggressive towards him. Henry conveniently worked two jobs and was rarely at home. Helga was forced to redirect her aggression which resulted in her getting into a fist fight with a neighbor.

When Henry refused to intervene, taking her side, she began attacking him. Henry questioning Helga's behavior insisted she see a psychologists. Upon seeing the psychologist Helga was diagnosed as having postpartum depression. Helga refused to get treatment for her depression stating that she could do it by herself. Henry began to notice a repeated pattern. Before long she was back drinking more than ever. Henry pled with her to seek counseling to get help for her anger management and alcohol dependency. Henry feared that Helga would hurt someone, or someone hurt her. Henry tried unsuccessfully to keep the peace in their home. Henry's refusal to give her any attention infuriated Helga, who beat him more.

Helga's abuse towards Henry had gotten out of control.

Henry dreaded coming home in fear of not knowing what to

expect. Henry had no one to confide in or any place to go for

support. Henry didn't have very many friends. Henry and

Helga had mutual friends from the tire plant. He feared what

would happen if rumors of the abuse ever got out. He was

concerned about how they would be viewed by their friends

and family. He worried about how the abuse would affect

their children. He was too ashamed to disclose to others the

ongoing mistreatment he was subjected to from his spouse.

Helga's physical abuse towards Henry made him feel less

than a man. Helga was a skilled fighter who stood six feet,

two inches, and was in good physical shape.

Henry knew that he could never hit a woman. He also knew that he could not continue to receive abuse at the hands of Helga. He feared either being hurt or hurting Helga. Henry worried that if he left her, he would not have anyone to look after the twins while he worked. In contrary, if he left her and didn't take the twins, he worried she would turn her aggression towards their children. Growing up in the church Henry knew how to pray if he knew nothing else. Henry wanted to keep his marriage together, he loved his wife and children dearly. However, Henry knew that he could not withstand very much more.

# HENRY'S PRAYER

Henry prayed to God expressing his marital concerns as he asked for guidance. Henry's prayer was as follows: Dear Lord, Prince of Peace, oh how I need thee in this hour. I need you now more than ever. My problem is much bigger than me. I no longer have peace in my home. The wife that you have given me and myself fight all the time. Lord of grace and mercy will you please remove my problem? I can no longer operate in such chaos and confusion. I know that God you are not the author of confusion, but of peace, as in all churches of the saints.

According to 1 Corinthians 14:33. I just want things back the way they used to be when I was a single man. He hears a steel soft voice speaking to him. Oh, my son, the woman you have, I did not give her to you. She was your choice for a wife. She is not your kingdom spouse. She was only meant to be in your life for a season. You never included me in your decision to marry her. My child, I instructed you to stand still, but you refused to take heed of my command. I am your father in heaven, and I know and see all. I warned you several times, but you failed to listen. I forgive you, my child, but you must suffer the consequences of your actions. Have faith in me, my child, and know that all is well.

The following day while playing outside the children noticed a strange man watching them. The stranger watched discreetly from the side of their home. The children immediately alerted Helga of the man's presence. Helga rushed out of the home in an attempt to investigate the stranger. Helga approached the stranger to inquire of the reason that he was lurking around their home. The stranger identified himself as a linemen with the electric company. He told Helga that he was given a work order to disconnect the electricity from the home for nonpayment. Helga knew that Henry was a wonderful provider and insisted that there must have been some type of misunderstanding.

Henry was also a wonderful family man and made every effort to take care of Helga and their children. Henry in fact many of times paid the bills before they became due. He didn't believe in being late and it was reflected in his credit score. Refusing to allow him to disconnect the electricity, she called to confirm the information provided by the engineer. She was surprised to learn that the bill was more than three months behind. Several payment arrangements had been set up on the account. However, no payments were ever made. The bill was more than two thousand dollars behind. She was speechless. She knew things were tough and many of the items that they once bought they could no longer afford.

However, she never knew just how tough things were.

Helga waited up to speak to Henry. When Henry got home,

she asked him why he didn't tell her that he hadn't paid the

electric bill. Reminding him that the electric bill is one of the

major bills in their home. Henry apologetically tells her that

he didn't want to worry her. Helga in a drunken rage begins

yelling at Henry. The couple has a big argument which

resulted in a physical altercation. Helga as usual began

pounding on Henry. He grabs her arm as she snatches away

from him, she loses her balance falling to the floor. Helga

accuses Henry of pushing her on the floor. Helga

immediately packed an overnight bag for herself and the

twins and left the family's home against Henry's wishes.

Helga's sister had recently moved into town where she had moved into her very first home. Helga told Henry she and the kids would be staying overnight at her sister's new home. Helga wrote her sister's new address on a sheet of paper, leaving it on a nightstand beside the couple's bed. Helga stated she would call Henry the following day after he had calmed down. Helga and the twins left the family's home never to be seen again. The following day Henry waited patiently to hear from Helga. He wanted to apologize to her and tell her how much he loved her and the twins and wanted them to come back home. The night passed and Henry never got a call from Helga.

The following day Henry located the paper that contained Helga's sister address, laying on the couple's nightstand. Henry was surprised to learn that the address of Helga's sisters' home was 333 Lovejoy Road. Helga wasn't from Poland and wasn't aware of the history of the home. Henry on the other hand was a native of Poland. Henry, like many of the town's people, had heard the rumors surrounding the home. He rushed over to the home where he knocked on the door, but his knocks went unanswered. He attempted to open the door, but the door was locked preventing him from entering the home.

He now feared for his family. Henry visited the home

day and night daily for a six-month time span, but no one

ever came to the door. Soon a year would pass, and he still

had not heard from Helga. Henry's life began to go in a

downward spiral. He knew deep down inside that he would

never see his family again. He tried to remain optimistic but

as time passed it became too much for him. He questions

how he and his family could have become victims of the

Mystical House. Henry was quickly reminded of the prayer

that he prayed a day prior to the disappearance of his family.

He was heartbroken to think that he could have possibly

brought such misfortunate event on his family by his selfish

prayers. He blamed himself for Helga and their children's

disappearance. He believed that the argument might have

been avoided if he had paid the electric bill. Angrily, he

turned from God. Henry stopped praying at the time when he

needed to pray the most. He too soon began consuming large

amounts of alcohol to soothe his pain. He traveled from street

corner to street corner, where he hung out, drinking liquor

daily. Henry mourned for his family. He could not maintain

employment and would eventually lose everything that he

had worked hard for.

He eventually found himself homeless. Henry tells officers that he finally had come to terms that his family was never coming back on the day he met Jennifer and Jaylyn Seahawk. Henry claims when he met Jennifer and Jaylyn Seahawk he was going to say his final goodbyes to his family. Henry presents the officers with a receipt for flowers and two plush animals that he bought and placed on the porch of the home as a memorial to his wife and kids. After learning of Henry's allegations, the mayor became even more concerned about his family's safe return. The mayor was afraid that his family was now the next victims of the Mystical House.

## THE ROOKIE

Henry and Mayor Seahawk were just two of the several residents who lost loved ones to the Mystical House. Others have come forward with similar stories about The Mystical House. A missing person's report was filed on behalf of both men for their loved ones. (Thirdly, the partner of the rookie took the microphone and testified to what he witnessed.) Officers decide to take things a step further. They decided to visit the Mystical House to conduct an investigation. They wanted to know the mysteries surrounding the home. After arriving at the home, law officials were unable to enter the house. A rookie police officer who had only been with the force for six months. He was looking to prove himself to his peers.

He made the decision to get permission to enter the home in search of the missing victims. After being granted permission, to entered the home against the advice of his fellow officers. The young rookie, after preparing to break down the front door, which had previously been locked. Upon checking the door a second time it magically opens when the doorknob is turned, unlocking the door. The others watched warily as the rookie entered the house. Two hours would pass before the rookie emerges from the home. His fellow colleagues were preparing to leave when the front door of *The Mystical House* popped opened. The officer appeared standing bewildered and dazed. He looked as if he had seen a ghost.

When asked what had taken place inside of the residence. He appeared shaken and distraught, before clutching his chest and collapsing. The officer was rushed to the hospital where he was examined. The rookie is believed to have suffered a heart attack. The officer who as a child was diagnosed with a heart murmur and currently seeks treatment. It was discovered during his examination that the rookie had not had a heart attack but oddly the heart murmur no longer exist. It is speculated that the chest pain he experienced during his visit in *The Mystical House* was the heart murmur being healed. While at the hospital the officer regained consciousness.

He was reluctant to speak about the events that had taken place inside the home. He was later released from the hospital. The following day when the officer didn't show up for work his partner went by his home to check on him. Only to find he had packed his belongings and left town, leaving a letter behind. The letter read as follows: It wasn't until my encounter in *The Mystical House* that my life was changed. I was shown some of the mysteries surrounding human existence. It wasn't until going into *The Mystical House* that I came to learn who I am as a person. In my learning who I am as a person I also learned the purpose for which I was created.

In order for one to know what they was created to do they must truly know their creator. In closing it was the best experience of my life and one that I will never forget. I must go fulfill the works that has been assigned to me by my Lord and Savior. The rookie has left behind his uniform to include his badge and gun that were assigned to him. The rookie unexpectedly left his custom-made pistol behind as well. He stated that he no longer needed the weapon and wished to gift it to his partner. He was never seen or heard from again. The mayor tries to remain hopeful now, feeling discouraged. He continues to pray for the safe return of his wife and son.

# WARNING BEFORE DESTRUCTION

Two years would pass, and there was still no sign of Jennifer and Jaylyn as the case grew cold. (Lastly, Jerry Nuttz is called to the podium where he shares his experiences. He will attempt to explain the mysteries surrounding *The Mystical House.*)

*The Mystical House* would soon get its next tenant. Jerry Nuttz had recently moved into town where he rented the property located at 333 Lovejoy Road. Jerry was the new jeweler in town. Jerry was a businessman by day and jewel thief by night. He was the rang leader of a jewelry heist.

He organized and employed the neighborhood gangsters to rob innocent bystanders for their jewels. In addition to breaking into homes in affluent communities, the gangsters also committed robberies at gunpoint. They were armed and dangerous and cared about nothing or no one. Jerry's main and only goal was to obtain wealth. He would destroy anyone who got in his way. Jerry felt as if he were invincible. One Friday, after a slow week at his jewelry store, Jerry decided to organize a jewel heist. He had high hopes of getting his hands on some valuable pieces of jewelry. Jerry planned a heist in a desperate attempt to boost sales at his store.

He stood in the living room of the home where he and

the three neighborhood gangsters plotted the theft. In the

process of organizing the crime, they never anticipated what

would happen next. They heard a calm, firm voice saying,

thou shalt not kill, thou shalt not steal, and thou shalt love

their neighbor just as thou self. (Exodus 20:13-15;

Matt.22:39) They all stopped and looked at one another.

Jerry, without question, was sure that they too had heard the

voice. Jerry, as well as the other crooks, turned around to find

out where the voice had come from. They noticed that no one

was there, at least as far as they could see. Gangster number

one, upon hearing the voice, fell to his knees.

Recognizing the voice as the voice of God. He began sobbing uncontrollably, and he immediately repented of his sins. He accepted Christ as his personal savior. Afterwards, he immediately departed from *The Mystical House*, advising his friends to do the same. Gangster number two, refusing to take heed, decided he wanted to execute the robbery exactly as it was originally planned. The third gangster decided with a heavy heart that he must be loyal to his friend. Jerry had participated in numerous jewelry heists, but this time it was different. Something deep within him was telling him not to take part in the theft. As the ringleader and the one who devised the scheme, he felt compelled to carry out the crime.

Jerry, along with two of the three men, decided to rob a house in one of the town's affluent areas. The men ignored all of the warning signs that were given to them, just as they had ignored the voice of God. The getaway van failed to start just as the men were preparing to leave *The Mystical House*. After working on the van for 45 minutes, it finally started. However, it ran hot on the way out of the neighborhood. The men than stole a van from a nearby convenient store. After arriving at the first neighborhood, the men were unable to get onto the property. The gate, which was normally open, was now closed, with a security guard working the entrance. Gangster number three knew that this was a sure sign that he should walk away and never look back.

He contemplated how he would break the news to his friend that he didn't want to take part in the robbery. However, he worried about what his friend might think of him. In the meantime, the men decided to case out the neighboring property. They spotted a home they knew would be a sure win for them. They were able to see the home's furnishings through the window from the street. They were confident they could sell the furnishings without any issues. The men were preparing to enter the home when they noticed that the homeowners were inside. The men had to quickly regroup. As the men were riding around the neighborhood, they soon spotted another home.

The second home was just like the first. They were able to view the home's interior through the window from the street before entering it. When the men arrived at the house, they were able to enter it without any issues. The inside of the home was very stylish and contained expensive pieces of furniture. They heard the voice once more as they were leaving the house: thou shalt not kill, thou shalt not steal, thou shalt love thou neighbor as thou love thou self. Jerry knew that he had made a mistake going into the home, but he felt that it was now too late. Jerry and gangster number three decided it would be best to leave the items behind and exit the home. Upon realizing they were inside the house, the second gangster refused to leave empty-handed.

He insisted they go on with the robbery as planned.

After loading their van to its full capacity with the stolen

items, they exited the neighborhood. The van rolled through a

red light, and blue lights came on behind it. The men spotted

the police in the rear-view mirror. They knew that they could

not stop. The van was not only stolen but also contained

stolen merchandise. Their refusal to stop led the police on a

high-speed chase. The high-speed chase ended in a crash,

overturning the vehicle. The driver of the vehicle gangster

number two, hardening his heart and refusing to hear the

voice of God, was killed instantly upon impact.

The third gangster, who did not follow his heart, sustained major injuries. He was hospitalized for a month before being discharged to begin serving his jail sentence. The accident left him a quadriplegic for the rest of his life. Jerry, the mastermind behind the operation, suffered severe head trauma. Jerry was admitted to the hospital's intensive care unit, where he was placed on life support. He was in a coma for six months before being released to the county jail. He returned to his residence at 333 Lovejoy Road following his release from custody. Jerry soon moved after returning to his residence. He felt he was not worthy of residing in the Mystical House. Jerry hasn't been the same since his incident.

His medical records indicate that he suffered significant head trauma, identifying the reason for his visits to the psychiatric ward. As a result of his injury, no one takes him seriously because of his mental health. Jerry can be seen daily standing on the street corner near the local eatery, where he preaches about the goodness of Christ Jesus. He constantly warns people about the coming of the "Messiah." Jerry never passes up an opportunity to share a word from Christ with the town's people. He tells people that his stay in *The Mystical House* is an experience that he will never forget. He gives thanks to God for using something so simple as *The Mystical House* to save his life.

# REVEALING THE MYSTERY

64

Jerry explains that *The Mystical House* is a real-life version of the bible. He explains that the house is mystical because it is a portal to travel in different time zones. The thirty rooms in the house, he says, are in different time zones. He explains that each time zone is a in a different dimension which happens to be an obstacle course dedicated to biblical teachings. The rooms are designed with obstacle courses to teach different life lessons. The rooms are structured around biblical laws and commandments as their central theme.

He contends that one must comprehend God's laws and commandments in order to fully comprehend the mystery surrounding them. He clarifies that not everyone will be able to enter the home. Jerry justifies a single person's admission to *The Mystical House*. He simply states that only those who are actively living in sin are permitted inside the home. Those who receive access to *The Mystical House* will be found guilty of their transgressions. Anyone may freely choose to enter the home. However, to leave the house, an individual would have to successfully pass the house's obstacle courses. Those granted access to the home will only be granted access to those rooms with obstacle courses designed specifically for their sins.

Each room coincides with a particular time zone. They will be faced with a series of events teaching them how to effectively deal with their problems without being in sin. An example would be a person who struggles with alcohol dependency. That individual may be placed in a time zone where they may be employed as a bartender. That individual will be forced to maintain their sobriety while affectively dealing with lives trials and tribulations. In order for a person to effectively pass a test of such caliber. They must implement biblical practices into their lives. When being presented with the question as to how long can an individual expect to remain in *The Mystical House.*

Jerry's response to the question is that it depends on the individual and how long it will take them to learn the lesson that's being taught. He explains that it also depends on the number of life lessons an individual will need to perfect before going to their next level. According to Jerry an individual will be held in a particular room until they can successfully pass the test. Once a person has understood and perfected God's commandments and laws then they will be allowed to leave *The Mystical House*. The front door of *The Mystical House* will no longer be locked preventing an individual from leaving. Jerry explains how many people oppose to leaving the home after completing the obstacle courses.

He explains how the presence of God can be felt in the home. It is because of God's presence that many people's lives are changed. According to the gospel of Psalms 16:10-11. God loves his children so much he will not leave his children's souls in hell, nor will he allow his holy ones to see corruption. He shows us the path of life and in his presence is fulness of joy. It is impossible to be in God's presence and not be a changed individual. Many people after leaving the home have a better relationship with Christ Jesus and seeks after him. They understand his commandments and laws, applying them to their daily lives. In term making the house a very favorable place to live.

One year in the home feels like but an hour. The strong presence of God surpasses all understanding and an abundance of peace. When asked about the owner of *The Mystical House*. Jerry stated that God was displeased with the fallen hero's cousin for selfishly using the medical center as his very own home. The gentleman was told to renovate the medical facility to bring it up to standards so that it may continue to help those in need. The cousin of the fallen hero decided upon completion of the project to use the facility for his personal gain preventing those needing medical treatment from receiving it. He too was locked into the house because his heart wasn't pure.

He was convicted of being selfish, self-centered, self-righteous, showing self-glorification, dishonest, deceptive, and disobedient. He was made to participate in several obstacle courses to gain access out of the house. Upon leaving *The Mystical House* he returned to his native homeland in Australia where he lived until his death. Jerry warns that once an individual has completed the obstacle courses in the Mystical House. After leaving the home the doors of the house will no longer be opened to that individual again. Those who are saved may not be allowed entry into the house because they have already perfected the obstacle courses.

Once the obstacle courses of *The Mystical House* are mastered the next step would be to work on the outside of the home bringing lost souls to Christ. Jerry frequently worked with the victims of *The Mystical House* and their loved ones. He encourages them to remain optimistic in the absence of their loved ones. After members of the committee hears Jerry's explanation of *The Mystical House*. Many questions his sanity while others believe him. Mayor Michael Seahawk and others refuse to have the house demolished. They felt as if destroying the home would destroy all possibilities of ever finding the truth of the mysteries surrounding the home.

They all felt as if solving the mysteries surrounding the house would provide more insight about the disappearance of its tenants. The mayor remained hopeful of someday being reunited with his wife and son. He prayed that if Jerry were correct that one day his wife and son would reemerge from the home. The towns people had mixed emotions about *The Mystical House*. There are some that believe Jerry's mythical story while others thinks he is insane. However, everyone can attest that there was some strange activity surrounding the home. At the towns meeting in deciding the fate of *The Mystical House*.

After hearing everyone from the town's mayor to the town's drunk testimonies about *The Mystical House*. It was decided upon unanimously not to remove the home from the town's historical list, preventing it from being demolished. It was decided upon to have the house removed from all realtors' listing, preventing it from being leased as one's personal residence. It was suggested the home be utilized only as a part of the town's history restricting entry. The committee makes one shocking discovery. Jerry informs the committee that the key to *The Mystical House* is useless. He explains that having the key does not guarantee entry to the home nor does locking the door prevents it.

The committee comes to the conclusion to have a barbwire fence placed around the home preventing entry to the home. The committee concluded their meeting. Upon the conclusion of the town's meeting about the fate of *The Mystical House* a week later Henry disappeared. There were rumors that Henry had finally gained entry into *The Mystical House*. While others speculate that he had moved out of state to get a fresh start in life. The mayor on the other hand never stopped searching for answers in the disappearance of his wife and son. There wasn't a day that went by the that he didn't think about his family. He constantly told himself that he was in a bad dream, and it would all soon be over. The mayor occasionally visited *The Mystical House* hoping to gain entrance into the home.

The day that his wife and son went missing he felt as if a part of him died. The mayor began attending church services on the regular. He prayed to God to give him another chance to make things right with his family. Upon his prayer to God although he did not have his family, he felt that everything was going to be fine. Mayor Michael Seahawk worked on putting his life back together. A year and five months would pass. One night as the mayor lay in the bed asleep. He smells what seems to be the smell of bacon spreading throughout his home. The mayor was sure he was dreaming as usual. However, this time the smell seemed more prominent than the last time.

He ignores the smell as he continues to sleep. He then smells what seems to be fresh cinnamon rolls. He remembered how Jennifer could make cinnamon rolls from scratch that would melt in your mouth. He immediately thought about his family and how he missed them and his wife's cooking. When the mayor got up for a drink of water. He enters the kitchen where he immediately notices Jennifer and Jaylyn sitting at the kitchen table eating breakfast. He thinks that his eyes are playing tricks on him. He wipes his eyes and refocus glancing over at the kitchen table again. It is clearly Jennifer and Jaylyn sitting at the table eating. Jennifer and Jaylyn runs over to him as the trio hugs and cries in one another's arms. Michael can't believe what he is seeing.

He immediately falls to his knees where he thanks God for answering his prayers. He is grateful to God for allowing him and his family to be reunited. The trio spends the remainder of the night conversating about *The Mystical House* as they share their experiences with Michael. Jennifer and Jaylyn confirms Jerry's claims of *The Mystical House.* Jennifer tells Michael that she had also met Henry's wife Helga and children in *The Mystical House.* Jennifer tells Michael that Helga had sent a message for Henry. Helga wanted Henry to know that she was sorry for her actions. She also wanted him to know that she and their children would be home soon.

Michael tells Jennifer he has not seen or heard from Henry in over a year and a half. He explains that Henry had gone missing a week after the committee's meeting. There were rumors that Henry had finally gained entry into *The Mystical House*. While others speculate that he had moved out of state to get a fresh start in life. Jennifer tells Michael that she could attest that Henry didn't gain entry into *The Mystical House*. Michael asks Jennifer if it were possible that Henry could have been in *The Mystical House*, and she have not known? Jennifer tells Michael that everyone that has ever gained entry into the home names are listed on a screen inside the home.

It also lists the date, time, and sins committed by the individual. Confirming that Henry wasn't in *The Mystical House*. Michael was excited to be able to give Henry the news that his wife and children were still alive and would be home soon. Michael set out to look for Henry. After a thorough research he learned Henry had moved out of state six hours away. Michael was able to get Henry's phone number where he reached out to him. Michael phoned Henry stating that he had some good news that he wanted to give him. He felt it was only appropriate to give it to him in person. Henry shared his address with Michael.

Henry told Michael that he too had some good news to share with Michael and would be looking forward to seeing him. Mayor Seahawk and his family aborded an airplane to see Henry. Upon arriving at Henry's house the Seahawks and Henry were both surprised. Henry was surprised when he opened the door and not only saw Michael but also Jennifer and Jaylyn. Henry was speechless. Michael told Henry well this is your surprise." Jennifer and Jaylyn has returned home from *The Mystical House* and Jennifer has a message for you. Henry was happy but surprised to see Jennifer and Jaylyn. Henry now realized that Jerry's story of *The Mystical House* was true after all.

Henry realizes that if Jerry's story is true and Jennifer and Jaylyn is now back that maybe Helga, and his children will be back as well.  Jennifer confirms what Henry is thinking. She tells Henry that Helga and their children are doing fine. Informing Henry that Helga and their children were almost finished with their last obstacle course. Jennifer tells Henry they are enjoying the obstacle courses and wishes he could join them in the house. Henry looks on in disbelief. Henry just as several others secretly looked at Jerry as being mentally unstable while many mocked him. Michael questions Henry well aren't you happy? Henry tells Michael and Jennifer that he is thrilled they are coming home. However, he has since moved on with his life.

Henry tells the Seahawks that his present to them were that he had remarried a year ago after declaring Helga and his children deceased. Although Henry loved Helga and their children, he knew that he couldn't have a relationship with her. Judy was his kingdom spouse and completed him in every way. Henry was the happiest he had ever been. Henry explains that in the beginning he blamed himself for Helga and his children's disappearance. Henry no longer blames himself for his family's disappearance. He now knows that it was for the best. Henry and his new wife had now been married for one year and a half. Everything was finally looking up for Henry. The newlyweds a few weeks before tying the knot signed the paperwork on their new home.

They were in the process of buying their first home.

Judy had sold her home to move out of state to make a fresh

start with Henry. His life was yet again turned upside down

just as he thought things had gotten back on track. Henry had

to prepare for the unexpected. Henry feared possibly losing

his new wife. He knew that if Jennifer was correct. Helga and

their children would be looking to reunite with him very

soon. He had no idea what he would tell his new bride or

how she would feel. He knew he had to think of something

quickly. Henry struggles as he looks for a way to tell Judy

that Helga and his children were still alive.

Henry contemplated how he would tell his wife about the events surrounding his family's disappearance and if she would believe him. Henry bought Judy a beautiful bouquet of yellow roses as they were her favorite flowers. When Judy got home after presenting her with the flowers. He sat her down telling her that he had something very important to talk to her about. Henry reminds Judy that he was married before they met. It was after the disappearance of his wife and children that he filed and was granted a divorce. Henry tells Judy that he had just received some information from a trusted source. It was shared with him that his wife and children were still alive and well.

Henry poured Judy up a cup of hot tea as he sits her down explaining to her all the details surrounding his family dynamics and the incident leading up to their disappearance. Henry notices that Judy doesn't seem surprised by the news. Henry asks her if she had heard what he had just said? Judy tells him that the information that he provided to her the Lord had already given to her prior to their meeting. Judy tells Henry that his ex-wife and children would be coming back to see him to let him know that they are all fine. She explained to Henry that everything would be fine. Informing Henry that Helga is only coming to make peace with him. Henry felt relieved after receiving the information provided by Judy and knowing that she was okay with it all.

Four weeks would pass before Judy and Henry received the visit that they had anticipated. It was on a Saturday at noon. Henry was watching television and Judy was catching up on minor housework. They heard the doorbell ring followed by a knock on the door. Henry and Judy met at the door where they stared at one another briefly before opening the door. Henry had a gut feeling that it was the visit they had been patiently anticipating. Upon opening the door Henry was stunned by the resemblance of the young teen. Henry felt as if he was looking in the mirror.

There stood a young boy who looked a lot like Henry in his youthful years. Henry was pleasantly surprised to learn it was Alex and Alexandria. The trio embraced one another for several minutes where they cried tears of joy. Henry notices Helga and a gentleman as they sits in the car looking on. Henry goes out to the car to speak with Helga. They immediately embraces one another. She apologizes to Henry for the way she treated him. Henry likewise apologized to her. Helga tells Henry that being in *The Mystical House* has taught her a lot. Henry tells Helga that he has heard a lot in general about *The Mystical House*. Henry tells Helga that he has something that he must tell her.

# THE WEDDING

Helga tells Henry that she too also has some things that she must discuss with him as well. Helga tells Henry that being in the house a lot was revealed to her about herself and life in general. She tells him that she had also learned that she and Henry were only meant to be together for a season. She and Henry wasn't meant to be together for the remainder of their lives. Helga hesitantly tells Henry that during her stay in *The Mystical House* she found her kingdom's spouse. Helga turns and introduces Henry to Harry, her fiancé. She tells Henry that he had proposed to her, and she has accepted the proposal. Henry starts to laugh as he is relieved.

He tells Helga I was going to tell you the very same thing. However, I am remarried and have been married for one year and a half now. The two began to laugh as Henry introduces Helga to Judy. Helga and Judy hit it off instantly. The couples became the very best of friends despite their pass. The time had finally come for Harry and Helga's wedding. Harry and Helga were preparing to go down the aisle. As they worked to finalize the details of their wedding. Henry and Judy are invited to participate in the wedding ceremony. Helga asked Henry to give her away at her wedding to Harry. Judy was one of Helga's bridesmaids. Helga and Harry had a beautiful wedding ceremony overlooking the lake.

The couple chose to implement the color scheme of The Mystical House into their wedding since it was where they first met. Henry and others could see an enormous change in Helga. He knew that whatever took place inside of *The Mystical House* impacted her life for the better. He knew that her stay in *The Mystical House* was the best thing that could have ever happened to her.

In attendance at Helga's wedding were several of her and Henry's old friends from the tire plant. Many of which found it odd to see her with someone other than Henry. Also in attendance at the wedding were Michael and Jennifer Seahawk and Jerry Nuttz.

At Helga's wedding reception Helga tossed her bouquet in the air only to have the guest accompanied by Jerry Nuttz to the wedding catch it. Everyone wished them luck as Jerry smiled and nodded in approval.

In conclusion: Alex and Alexandria now not only had their parents back in their lives. They had stepparents that loved them just as their very own parents. They were the true definition of an extended family.

Jennifer Seahawk helped Harry and Helga find a home. Henry helped Harry to establish employment. *The Mystical House* was kept only as a part of the town's history.

Michael and Jennifer Seahawk made it a point to never leave their home mad with one another. They also decided to never make important decisions without consulting one another.

The state decided to build another medical facility next to *The Mystical House.* They hoped to have the same success as the previous medical facility. Jerry continued on his journey working to bring lost souls to Christ.

# THE END

# AUTHOR'S PAGE

My name is DeiAdra NiCole E., for clarification, it saddens me that others will take credit for another individual's work. However, without any further delay. I *must* thank my heavenly father, everything that I am is all because of his grace and mercy. I didn't think that I would see the day that I would be publishing my third book. God has really been good to me. It is my prayer that this book will be a blessing to those who reads it. It is also my prayer that this book will be used to encourage, uplift, and motivate someone in their time of need. I am also working to self-publish three children's books and two adult books. I truly want to thank everyone for their support. If no one has told you that they love you on today. Please, know that God loves you and so do I. Until next time. Be Blessed!!!